L.E. Miller

Drama in The Hood
A Cliché Series Book One

Chapter 1

Another day in the hood. The streets ran with your thugs, street nigga's and the fast ass round the way girls looking for a quick come up. It was afternoon, and the sun was high in the sky. Keith was sound asleep with an arm draped over his eyes to keep the peaking sun from waking him through the blinds.

"Yo Keith wake up!" Tavon said as he burst into the room.

He was already sipping on a drink apparent from the red plastic cup in his hand. Keith was a light sleeper, so he heard his brother's demand yet chose to lay there and pretend to be sleep. Tavon stood over his brother deciding to be a dick he licked his finger and gave him a wet willy, knowing his little brother wasn't sleeping. Keith sat up wiping his ear out as his brother looked at him amused by his actions.

"What the hell?" Keith bellowed.

"Get up! We going to the mall." Tavon said as he continued to sip his drink.

Keith sucked his teeth before turning his back to his brother and pulling the sheet over his head. "Five more minutes" Keith said from under the sheet.

"Yeah, whatever." Tavon said annoyed walking out the bedroom as Sean was making his way up the stairs.

"Is he getting ready?" Sean asked as he made it to the top landing of the steps.

"Nope!" Tavon said before attempting to finish off his dink.

Sean snatched it from him before bursting into his little brother's room and throwing the contents on him. Keith jumped from his bed wet and sticky from the alcohol in the cup and furious.

"What the hell is wrong with you?!" He screamed as his brother. Tavon and his older cousin Mike stood at the bedroom door laughing.

"Get dressed so we can go. Now!" Sean said before walking out slamming the door behind him.

***

'Ding dong'

The sound of the doorbell chimed through the house alerting Lizzy who was in the basement watching television and waiting for her sister to finish getting ready. She ran up the stairs and answered the door to see Erick standing there looking sexy as usual. Lizzy always had a crush on him but never said anything because he was her sister's friend.

"What you are doing here?" Lizzy asked trying her hardest not to blush.

"Well damn! I don't get a 'Hey Erick'?" he said grinning.

Lizzy cracked a smile as she moved to the side to allow Erick to enter before she closed the door. "Nope." Lizzy said jokingly.

"Alright. I see how you going to treat me." Erick said chuckling "Where Sabrina?"

"Getting ready you know she takes forever." Lizzy said as they both proceeded to the basement to wait for Sabrina.

"Want a freeze pop?" Lizzy asked as Erick plopped down on the sofa.

"Sure" Erick says.

Lizzy retrieves two freeze pops from the deep freezer and proceeds over to the computer desk to open them with the scissors. As she stood there with her back to him, Erick took that chance to stare at her ass until the silence was broken.

"Sabrina told me you got accepted to Morgan." Lizzy said as she walked over and sat next to him on the sofa, passing him the freeze pop.

"Yeah, I got accepted to Capitol and Bowie too." He said biting into the cold treat.

Lizzy took a bite of her freeze pop before continuing her line of questioning.

"So where are you going?" she asked continuing to eat.

Erick shrugged, he had a mouth full of freeze pop and he honestly had no idea where he wanted to go.

"I don't know." he said after swallowing what was in his mouth. They finished the frozen treats and Lizzy discarded the packages in the trash.

"Can I ask you something?"

Lizzy asked as she returned to the sofa. The sofa was perfect for two people, yet they were practically sitting on top of each other.

"Yeah sure." Erick said.

He was leaned back on the sofa against the armrest. His gaze going back and forth from the television and Lizzy. Lizzy sat back on the sofa and crossed her legs. Which caused Erick to shift in his seat. Her long caramel legs and thick thighs sat perfectly in her denim shorts.

"Do you think I'll fit in at Edmondson?" she asked. The question caused Erick to turn and look at her puzzled.

"Yeah. Why?" he asked looking concerned. He never knew Lizzy to be insecure, so the question caught him off guard.

"I'm just scared of transferring schools. All my friends are at Patterson and it took me forever to shed that nerd cliché there. I just don't feel like starting over." She confessed.

Lizzy was a nerd, but she was also sexy, alluring and intelligent. Erick scanned her body from her soft caramel legs to her thick thighs, small waist and to her amazing rack that sat high in her knitted-V-neck shirt. Finally settling on her beautiful face and her beautiful hazel eyes that hid behind a pair of black framed glasses. She noticed him noticing her and secretly ate it up.

"Trust me. You will fit in perfectly." Erick finally said licking his lips.

Sabrina came down the stairs with her house keys and purse dressed casually in a pair of slim fit blue denim jeans, all white shell top Adidas and a yellow off the shoulder blouse that showed her small butterfly tattoo above her left breast. "Hey, Erick. I'm ready?" she said turning off the television.

***

An inpatient Darnell stood at the front door of the house waiting for his sister. "Janay, hurry your butt up!" he yelled up the steps.

Janay finally appeared from her room and made her way down the stairs. Darnell immediately looked her up and down shaking his head in disapproval. "Why do you always have to dress like a damn slut?" he barked.

Janay was sporting a pair of all white Air Forces, denim dark blue shorts that hugged her hips and round ass and a white crop top that showed her pierced mid-drift. She rolled her eyes at her brother's comment. "Can we go? She said crossing her arms. Janay was spoiled. Their parents let her do whatever she desired, and it was her brothers' job to check her ass when she got out of line. Not feeling like arguing, Darnell

shook his head and pulled the front door open and they

proceeded to go meet up with the rest of the crew.

***

Mondawmin mall was bustling with people young and

old getting ready for the new school season. Darnell and Erick

spotted the game store and parted from the girls. As soon as

Darnell walked into the store his attention went straight to the

pretty girl behind the counter.

"Damn." He said to himself as he grabbed a random

game and approached the counter.

The young lady picked up the game and giggled as she

looked from the game to Darnell. "SpongeBob? Aren't you a

little too old for that?" She asked still giggling. Darnell looked down at the game and smiled at the embarrassing random

choice.

"Oh, I didn't mean to pick that up." Darnell said

smiling.

The cashier placed the game behind the counter as

Darnell moved to the side to allow the kid behind him to check

out. He watched the young lady behind the register intently.

"You look familiar." He finally said as the customer grabbed

his bag and left.

"I knew you wouldn't remember me." She said coming

from behind the counter. Darnell soaked in her body, she filled

out her uniform quite well.

"So, I have met you before?" Darnell asked trying to

think back.

She laughed at the puzzled look on his face. "Remember

eleventh grade? I had glasses, I was fat, I always wore black?"

Darnell's eyes widened when he realized who she was.

"Kayla?" he blurted out. He was shocked. Summer had done

her damn good. "Wow, you look great." He said as they gave

each other a hug.

"Thanks." Kayla said as she went back behind the

counter to ring customers. She pulled a piece of receipt tape

after her customer and jotted her number down and handed it

to Darnell. "Hit me up sometime." Kayla said smiling. She

checked out Erick and Darnell shot her a wink before they

both left the store.

The girls found themselves walking into Foot Locker

where Sabrina and Janay caught the eye of two young male

employees working the sales floor. James tapped Christopher who was already looking in the direction of Sabrina.

"She can get it." He said smiling. His cockiness on full display. James felt he was God's gift to the universe and wasn't shy to admit it.

"Which one you talking about? They both pretty." Christopher said. He was examining Sabrina in particular. Of the two girls, he could tell she was the shy one and that piqued his interest even more than her beauty.

"The one in the shorts." James said licking his lips.

Sabrina turned from the wall of shoes and noticed the boys staring in their direction. She tapped Janay who was still looking at the wall.

"What?" Janay said looking at her friend. Sabrina

gestured over to the boys who were still admiring their beauty.

"Damn, he fine." Janay said giggling. Sabrina laughed with

her then caught up with her sister who was in the men's

section looking at sneakers.

James took the opportunity to approach Janay who went

back to looking at the sneakers. "Hi, would you like some help

looking..." James trailed off as he watched Janay bend over in

front of him. She knew exactly what she was doing as she

turned to face him. "My names James. What's yours?"

"Janay." She said smiling hand on her hip. Janay craved

attention from the opposite sex and learned at an early age how

to use her body to get it.

James liked what he saw and the smile on his face showed that. He was a pretty boy and oozed swag. His almond skin was damn near perfect despite the tattoo he sported on his neck. He stood a few feet taller than Janay at 5'8" which wasn't a big task due to her petite stature of 5'4".

"You have a man?" James asked not wasting any time. He always went after what he wanted and was starting to think this summer was going to end on a low note until now.

"Not at the moment." Janay said flirtatiously.

The moment was interrupted by James boss yelling across the store for him to get back to work.

"She a bitch." James said referring to his boss. Janay giggled. James reached into his pocket to retrieve his cell phone. "So, can you plug those digits in? A nigga got to get back to making this money to take your fine ass out." He said cracking a smile.

Janay snatched the phone and saved her number in it before catching up with Sabrina and Lizzy allowing James to get back to work.

James walked inside the warehouse to see Christopher coming down the ladder with a shoe box "Guess what?" James said showing all thirty-two teeth. Chris stepped off the ladder and gave James a quizzical look. "I got shorty number."

Christopher snickered "You always get some girl number. Hoe ass." He said chuckling.

"Because I'm a player. Don't hate." James said brushing off his shoulders. He clearly was feeling himself.

"Yeah in your mind. I'm going back to work."

Christopher said walking around James and out the warehouse.

Chris presented the box of sneakers to Lizzy who had taken a

seat on the bench to try them on. Sabrina noticed Christopher

catching quick glances at her, yet she chose to ignore it. She

was the opposite of Janay. Where Janay craved attention, she

could do without. Which was hard due with her beauty. Even

when she called herself dressing down, she still commanded

attention. Her jet-black hair stopped just above her full round

butt and her light skin complimented the ruby red lipstick she

loved to sport.

"Do you want them?" Sabrina asked her little sister. She

was ready to go, and stop being admired so much by the boy

helping them.

"Yeah." Lizzy said placing them back in the box and sliding her sneakers back on.

"Alright. Take them off and give them to…"

Chris interrupted Sabrina to give his name.

"Christopher" he said smiling a little. He checked them out at the register and shot Sabrina a flirtatious wink as she walked away from him.

The girls ran into the boys who were coming around the corner. Erick immediately noticed the bag in Lizzy's hand.

"New kicks?" he asked.

"Yup. What you get?" Lizzy asked looking at his bag.

"The new 2k." Erick said.

They were walking together behind the group who made their way into Old Navy. Splitting up, Lizzy went with the boys. She wasn't into the whole shopping thing and she really didn't need anything clothes wise. Erick pulled out a pair of jeans. "What you think about these?" He asked Lizzy.

Lizzy frowned a little as she looked at his choice and quickly pulled a pair of dark denim wash jeans from the rack to counter. "They alright, but I think these will look better." Lizzy said taking the pair he chose and placing them back on the rack, handing him the new option. "Go try them on."

Darnell was a few feet away looking at polos listening and watching Lizzy and Erick's interaction. When his brother ran off to the dressing room he stopped and gave his full attention to Lizzy.

"What's going on with you two?" he asked catching Lizzy off guard.

Lizzy looked at him and rolled her eyes. "We're just friends. Damn!" Lizzy said clearly irritated by the question. She gave Darnell no chance to respond before jetting off to the dressing room area to wait for Erick.

Sabrina rummaged around the table that housed some jeans as Sean, Tavon, and Mike walked up behind her. "It's weird that we keep running into each other like this."

Sean said behind a sinister grin. The sound of his voice was unsettling to Sabrina as she turned to face him noticing he wasn't alone. The boys towered over her 5'6" frame and left no space for her to escape.

"What do you want?" Sabrina asked almost inaudible trying her best not to look them in the eyes.

"I want you back. Sean said brushing a hand across her

cheek before she pulled away in disgust.

"After what you did? Y'all did? I should have you all

locked up. Stay away from me or I will!" Sabrina barked

pushing Tavon and Sean apart to make her exit. They allowed

her to leave as Sean watched her hastily walk away.

Chapter 2

After the mall, they all went back to Erick, Darnell and Janay's house. Everyone split immediately, Sabrina and Janay went into the basement, Darnell went into the living room. Erick and Lizzy stood in the foyer in an awkward silence.

"Well, you ready for me to smash you in 2k?" Lizzy asked laughing.

"Bet!" Erick said looking surprised.

They disappeared up the stairs to go to his room. Darnell sat on the sofa shaking his head.

"Those two obvious as shit" he said to himself as he turned the tv on and stretched across the sofa.

Erick and Lizzy sat on the edge of his bed picking their teams. Before the game started Erick turned to face Lizzy.

"Let's make this game interesting." Erick said smiling.

Lizzy looked at him skeptical "What did you have in mind? Taking into consideration that you're about to lose." Lizzy asked while also stroking her ego.

Erick burst out laughing at her bold statement but loved her confidence. "When I win, I get to take you out on a date." He finally said.

Lizzy's eyes widened at his proposition and she sat there mulling it over. She could see Erick growing nervous from the silence.

"What do I get?" Lizzy finally asked breaking the silence.

Erick cleared his throat before responding. "Whatever you want you're going to lose anyway." He said smiling nervously. Erick had been crushing on Lizzy for some time and he knew that if he didn't shoot his shot than someone else would. Lizzy was seventeen going on eighteen in a month and he was nineteen, and they had been flirting with each other for about a year but never made a move.

Lizzy smiled as she stood and walked to the door. Erick's heart started to sink in his chest as he thought she was leaving, and he blew it. When she locked the door, he grew curious placing the controller down and standing up. Lizzy walked over to him and bit down on her bottom lip before she acted on what was going through her mind.

"Well, I guess I should get it now." Lizzy pulled him by his grey polo and kissed him softly on the lips before pulling away.

"Fuck that game." Erick said grabbing her by the waist and kissing her passionately.

Chapter 3

The first day of school is nothing special in the hood. It's just a five day a week daycare center for parents to have their kids go. Sabrina left her sister in the office to go use the restroom since the staff was taking their time getting Lizzy her schedule. As she walked down the hall face buried in her social media page, she didn't notice Sean was walking towards her. He allowed her to bump into him.

Sabrina attempted to apologize until she realized who it was, and she proceeded to turn around to go back to the office suddenly able to hold her bladder a little longer. Sean stepped in front of her blocking the path to escape, he always was a control freak.

"Bitch don't turn away from me!" he said. His voice full of irritation as he grabbed her arm. The halls were full of students mingling and trying to find their classroom that the altercation went unseen and the ones that did see it knew to stay out of it due to fear of Sean's wrath. He had a reputation and was not one to fuck with.

"Don't fucking touch me!" Sabrina said yanking her arm away. She hated Sean and his friends. Although her reasons were justifiable, she hated that she visibly showed that he got under her skin. *"I should have gone to the police"* she thought to herself before attempting to step around him.

Sean didn't appreciate that and yanked her arm pulling her back towards him.

"You still hard of hearing I see." Sean said anger surging through his body. His grip was iron as he stood over Sabrina and her eyes began to well up with tears.

"Hey, baby. You going to introduce me to your friend?" Christopher asked walking up beside Sabrina interrupting the altercation. He caught them both off guard as Sean dropped his grip on Sabrina to give Christopher his full attention.

"He's not my friend! More like a stalker psychopath ex!" Sabrina said. Her voice was filled with hate and Sean felt the venom as she spoke.

"Who the fuck is he!?" Sean said reaching to grab Sabrina once again. His stare was cold and lifeless. His jaw muscles clenched with anger and frustration.

Sabrina's body tensed when she saw him reach for her,

yet it was intercepted when Christopher stepped in front of her.

"Dude I suggest you walk away!" Christopher said sizing

Sean up. Sean was taller than him at 6'0" but he still was

willing and capable of beating his ass if he needed to.

"Or what?" Sean said looking at Christopher. Sean didn't

take to well to being challenged or being disrespected as his

gaze wandered to Sabrina who was positioned behind

Christopher. His eyes were soulless and gave her chills.

The altercation was cut short by the school's officer who

made the boys go their separate ways before blows were

thrown.

"Thank you so much, Christopher." Sabrina said as she

and Chris stood there.

Christopher smirked "You remembered my name huh? And don't mention it I know those type of guys and I can't stand them. You need to be more careful beautiful." Christopher said examining her arm noticing a bruise forming.

Sabrina self-consciously covered it "Well I should get back to my sister. Thanks again." She began to walk back to the office.

Christopher yelled after her. "Wait. What's your name?" Christopher asked.

Sabrina turned back and yelled her name to him before disappearing into the office.

"Sabrina!"

***

Sabrina walked into her English class and noticed

Christopher sitting at his desk drawing in his notebook. She

made her way to the desk next to his and had a seat placing her

books down. The gesture caused Christopher to look up from

what he was doing, and he smiled when he noticed it was

Sabrina. "Well, this has to be faith." He said.

Sabrina laughed and smiled at him just as the teacher

came in the class. Mr. Lucas was the English teacher a young

man recently out of college and ready to make a difference in

the world with teaching. The students smelled his freshness as

soon as he walked through the door. Attention went towards

him mostly from the female students, and the boys

immediately felt threatened.

Mr. Lucas stood at the front of the class and stared out at the sea of young adults. He wasn't naïve of his effects with women. Woman young and old seemed to get sucked into his good looks and charm. "Good morning class. My name is Mr. Lucas and I will be your English teacher." Mr. Lucas said turning towards the dry erase board behind him and writing his name on it. A few girls clustered in the back used that opportunity to make swooning noises towards him with whistles and a few 'he cute' loud enough for everyone to hear. Mr. Lucas turned back to address the class. "The person you're sitting next to now will be the person you will work with for the whole year.

Chris looked at Sabrina and smiled. "I can work with that."

The teacher continued to speak, focused on getting through the first-day direction as quickly as possible only to repeat to the next set of students for the next eight hours.

***

"Who in here has trouble in Geometry?" Ms. Drayton asked watching half the class raise their hand. It was no surprise to her at all. She began to walk around the classroom as she addressed the class. "I figured that." She said as she began to discuss the class syllabus an expectation. Janay and James immediately tuned her out and started having a quiet conversation amongst themselves. Which was quickly interrupted with the smack of a ruler on their desk causing them to almost jump out of their skin. "Let me make this perfectly clear. I don't appreciate anyone talking while I'm talking. If I catch you two talking again, I will put you out. The first day or not!" Ms. Drayton hissed. As she turned to walk away James decided to challenge her threat and opened his mouth.

"Damn, she needs a man in her life!"

The class including Janay laughed at the comment pissing Ms. Drayton off even more. "You two! Hallway now!" Ms. Drayton screamed. It was the first day and she could already see how the rest of the school year was going to go.

The hallways were empty due to students and administrators in class. James looked at Janay smiling devilishly as he pulled his car keys out his pocket along with a newly rolled blunt and held them in front of Janay. "Are you coming?" James asked. As if he already knew the answer he began to walk towards the exit of the school and Janay

followed closely behind. James sat in the driver's seat of his

father's 2018 Chevrolet Suburban in the schools parking lot.

Pulling out his cell phone he sent out a group text to his

brother who was still sitting in their homeroom class. *"Yo! Me*

and this shorty from work got put out of class lol. We going to

ditch, catch up with you later." Pressing send and tossing the

phone in the cup holder he turned the key to the ignition and

the truck roared to life.

"So, where we headed?" Janay asked as she put her cell

phone back into her bookbag and turned her attention to

James. James looked at her and smiled.

"Well, my peoples not home if you want to chill." He

said exiting the schools parking lot and heading in the

direction of home. Janay shrugged and set back in the

passenger seat while *'Drake's Child Play'* played through the

speakers.

Thirty minutes and a blunt later James and Janay pulled

up to his house. They exited the car and Janay followed closely

behind James who walked up the steps leading to his parent's

rowhouse. James unlocked the door and held it ajar allowing

Janay to walk in ahead of him, he took that time to check out

her ass one more time.

"That ass dangerous and you know it." James said closing

the front door behind them and locking it. Janay laughed at his

comment as she observed her surroundings before her eyes

came to a stop on James who was standing there looking sexy

as hell. James was light skin, skinny built, he stood 5'10" with

hazel eyes and a fresh shaped up fade. His smile was gorgeous

the day she met him in Foot Locker yet the gold fronts

he was rocking just made his smile even more alluring.

James walked into the living room and connected his phone to the Bluetooth speaker continuing the playlist from the car. While Janay made herself comfortable on the sofa as she watched him prep a new blunt for their consumption '*Rae Sremmurd Buckets*' played through the speakers as Janay started dancing in her seat. She was slightly high off the first blunt and was feeling herself more than usual, whipping her black eighteen inches from side to side as she danced to the music. James smiled and laughed enjoying the show as he lit the blunt. "Why are you sitting so far away?" James asked blowing the smoke into the air.

Janay stood and walked over to him grabbing the blunt from his hand and inhaling the contents. James admired her swag, a woman that looked good in anything was far and in-between. When he first met her, she left little to the imagination and now she stood in front of him dressed innocently in her navy slim cut jeans and a flirty pink blouse that wrapped her breast nicely. James pulled Janay down onto

his lap as she blew the smoke through her nose.

"You bad as shit, ma." James said squeezing her ass.

"You going to be my girl, right?"

Janay placed the blunt in his mouth and giggled. "I don't

think you could handle me." Janay said. She was cocky, but

she had just met her match. James sucked on the blunt for a

moment before responding his eyes tracing her body.

He blew the smoke to the side and licked his lips.

"That's where you're wrong. The question is can you handle

me." His bold statement along with the growth in his pants

caught Janay off guard and before she could come back with a

slick response James pulled her face towards him and kissed

her lips.

***

'Where is this girl?' Sabrina thought as she, Lizzy and

Erick stood outside of the school watching the doors waiting

for Janay.

"I'm thinking she found something or someone to occupy her time." Lizzy said air quoting the words 'something' and 'someone'.

"Aye!" Erick said trying to defend his sister knowing it could possibly be true.

Lizzy sucked her teeth and looked at him. "You know your sister is a hoe so don't try it." Lizzy said bursting out in laughter.

Erick shook his head, he had no words to combat that truth. All he could do was pull out his cell phone and call his sisters phone which went to voicemail after a few rings. Just as Erick put the phone back in his pocket Christopher came out the school with two other guys trailing behind him. Christopher spotted Sabrina and jogged over to her. Introducing himself to Erick and giving Lizzy a head nod. Erick and Lizzy put some space between Chris and Sabrina so they could talk. "Your girl not here." Chris said showing her his text from his brother. "She fell into the spell of my hoe ass brother." Chris said laughing.

Sabrina shook her head and laughed a little. "Her brother is going to kill her." She said taking the phone out of his hand and punching something into the screen before handing it back. "I just texted my phone. Please text me your address so I can send to her brother." Sabrina said as she turned to walk away and catch up with Erick, and Lizzy.

"Well don't tell her I'm the one that gave her up." Chris yelled after her laughing.

"I can't make that promise it's you or me." Sabrina yelled across the parking lot back at Christopher before getting in the back seat of Darnell's car with Lizzy.

***

Christopher walked into the house with his cousins closely behind. The smell of weed instantly hit their nose as they followed the music into the living room. Janay and James lay together on the sofa sleep and completely unaware of the boy's presence. Christopher smacked his brother lightly on the cheek to wake him up.

James opened his eyes and saw his brother staring down at him. "Get up. We bout to have company. Clean this shit up." Chris said as Janay finally awoke wiping her eyes which were red and low from the rotation session that happened prior to his arrival. Chris laughed at her presence "He gave you that good shit I see." Brian and David laughed before walking to the kitchen to freeload on their Aunts food.

"Who coming here?" James asked as he stood and stretched.

Chris began to walk up the stairs as he answered the question. "Janay brother." Chris said smiling. He was no cock blocker, but his brother was a slut there is no sugar coating it.

Janay jumped up from the sofa frantic and begin to fix herself up. "My eyes red?" She asked trying her best to widen her eyes. James tried his best not to laugh but wasn't successful. He fell on the sofa in laughter trying to catch his breath. Janay caught an attitude and grabbed her purse and rushed to the bathroom to get herself together. Darnell was worse than her parents. He was strict and overbearing and he wasn't hesitant on voicing his opinions on Janay's choices.

The knock on the door caused James to grab the evidence off the coffee table and place it into his pocket before answering the door. James tried his best not to look as high as he felt but he was a better actor in his mind than in reality. Sabrina laughed.

"I hope Janay don't look as high as you. Her brother will flip out." She said looking behind her. Darnell was walking up the walkway as she saw Janay rounding the corner and she noticed her best friend looking abnormal the closer she got to the front door. Sabrina pushed James to the side and grabbed Janay and pulled her back towards the direction she came. "I have eye drops in my purse. Bitch you need them."

Darnell walked up to the door and began to greet himself when he noticed James standing in the doorway. "Shit man it's been awhile" he said dabbing up James.

James moved to the side and allowed Darnell to enter the house before closing the door. Darnell walked into the living room and sat on the sofa observing his surroundings. "Janay!" Darnell yelled through the house.

James chuckled before he took out a blunt and lit it. He took a pull from the joint before offering some to Darnell who refused the offer. "I haven't smoked in two years man." Darnell said as Janay and Sabrina emerged from the bathroom. Janay looked better thanks to her Sabrina, but her brother wasn't stupid, and he knew she was high as a kite. Before Darnell could open his mouth to give her the third degree the front door opened, and Kayla walked through it. Darnell's attention went straight to her and so did hers as she smiled flirtatiously and dropped her backpack by the stairs. Kayla didn't go to Edmondson like the rest of them she went to another school across town that had mandatory sexy uniforms complete with the knee-high socks and school girl skirt. James cleared his throat as the two stared at each other for what seemed like forever.

Janay and Sabrina had made their way out of his line of fire and were now standing at the bottom of the stairs waiting for the awkward ogling to stop. James walked over to the girls blowing smoke out his nose as he got closer.

"Can I talk to my girl for a second?" James said grabbing ahold of Janay's hand and smirking.

The question caught Janay off guard "Your girl huh?" Janay asked letting out a giggle. James pulled Janay away and they went outside on the porch to paw at each other and spend a little more time together. Sabrina watched Darnell interact with Kayla and could clearly see he was interested and no longer interested in leaving so soon. The sound of a voice from the top of the steps caused Sabrina to turn her attention to see Christopher looking down on her and smiling.

"We have to stop running into each other like this." Sabrina said jokingly.

Chris proceeded down the stairs and stopped on the bottom landing. He had changed out of his clothes and was now wearing a pair of sweatpants and a wife beater. His body was tatted up. From his half sleeves to his chest. Sabrina was attracted for sure but wasn't going to make him aware of her interest in him just yet. "Well. I like our little run-ins." Chris said.

His attention was directed to the living room when he heard his sister laughing and to his surprise, he saw Darnell standing there. "Darnell!?" Chris yelled in his direction. He and Darnell used to run the streets together before he went away to Juvenile prison for three years. Darnell didn't even know he was out.

Darnell turned to the direction the familiar voice came from and was surprised to see Christopher standing there. "Oh shit. Boy, when you get out of jail?" Darnell asked walking

over to him to dab him up.

The mention of jail caused an immediate mood shift in

Sabrina that Chris noticed immediately.

"Been out for six months. Did my schooling in the inside so

luckily I was able to come out and be in the grade I'm

supposed to be in." Chris said occasionally glancing at Sabrina

who was now not making eye contact.

"Well, we need to catch up. I'm going to get my sister's

home and I'll get up with you soon. Darnell said pulling out

his car keys. Sabrina grabbed them from his hand and started

walking towards the front door.

"See you tomorrow Sabrina." Christopher said.

Sabrina opened the door and waved to him before heading

to the car. "Janay we're leaving now!" Sabrina said not

stopping her stride to the car.

Janay gave James a quick kiss then ran off behind her

best friend who was now sitting in the backseat pouting.

"What's wrong with you?" Janay asked looking back from the passenger seat.

"Nothing. Just want to go home." Sabrina said as Darnell took his place in the driver's seat and she gave him the keys. As they pulled off, she watched Chris and James standing on the porch talking.

"What was that about? James asked looking at his brother who was standing there with his hands in his pockets staring in the direction the car had disappeared in.

"Well, she just found out I was in jail. Let's just say she didn't take that well." Chris said before he walked back into the house leaving his brother standing on the porch.

***

Sean and his crew sat in the basement of his parent's home smoking weed. "Guess who in my class?" Tavon said passing the joint to his cousin Mike.

"Who?" Mike asked coughing on the smoke he was inhaling into his lungs.

"Sabrina" Tavon answered.

The joint made its way to Sean who head was laid back staring at the ceiling.

"I saw that bitch today." he said before inhaling the joint. "She has a little boyfriend." Everyone quieted as Sean took another pull from the joint and passed it.

"So, what does that mean?" Chad asked flicking the ash from the joint before inhaling.

Sean sat up and looked at him as if he asked a dumb question. "Well if I can't have her no one can."

Chapter 4

The routine was set, it was a normal high school day at Edmondson Westside. The bell's chime echoed through the halls as the teens and administrators disbursed to their scheduled classes. Janay who walked hastily towards her classroom notebook in hand was quickly intercepted by Sean who came from behind and pulled her into the stairwell with his brother and her ex-boyfriend Tavon. As he removed his had from her mouth Janay attempted to run away but was grabbed by Tavon so she couldn't get away.

"What do you want!?" she asked scared and pissed that they were in her presence.

"You still friends with Sabrina?" Sean asked as he towered over her. He got off on intimidating and demeaning girls however Janay was a firecracker and he never liked her snappy attitude or smart-ass mouth.

"She's moved on! So, I suggest you take the blessing of her not pressing charges on your trifling ass and leave her alone!" Janay said pulling out of Tavon's grip and starring Sean straight in the eye. "You actually think she would have lost her virginity to you? You really are fucking stupid!"

Sean smacked her and caused her to fall onto the floor. "You tell her I'll see her soon." He said before they walked away leaving her on the floor.

The timing to go to the restroom for Sabrina couldn't have been worse. As she left her classroom and walked towards the bathroom, she was unaware of the approaching danger that had rounded the corner as she entered the bathroom. Sean's jaw clenched as he proceeded towards the lady's room where Sabrina was. Anger and frustration written on his face. Sean stormed into the lady's room with no regards to where he was or who saw him.

Sabrina froze as she came out the stall and saw Sean standing there. His eyes were full of hate and she saw the same guy that raped her last summer. Regret and fear filled her. Regret that she didn't go to the police and fear that it was all about to happen again. As Sean stepped closer, Sabrina backed away until the bathroom wall stopped her from going any further. The tears began to roll down her cheek as he stepped closer and invaded her space.

"Help!" Sabrina screamed before Sean covered her mouth and pressed his body on hers.

His breath on her neck and the growth she felt in his jeans caused her to cry harder as she began to fight against his weight.

Sean punched her in the stomach causing her fights to seize. Grabbing her by her hair Sean forced her to look up at him and forced a kiss on his lips as he fondled her breast. Placing a firm hand around her neck as he stuck his free hand down her khaki pants and started rubbing on her vagina.

The sound of the lunch bell ringing cause Sean to pull his hand out of her pants.

"Your still mines." He said before forcefully kissing her and releasing her neck. He darted out the bathroom and didn't look back.

Sabrina locked herself in a stall and slid to the floor crying as her head fell into her lap. She felt defeated, hopeless and worthless.

Lizzy sat at a lunch table by herself eating her meal when Keith approached her with his Styrofoam tray of food. They had a few classes together and Keith was interested in getting to know the new girl. Lizzy had sparked his interest the very first day he saw her so he wanted to shoot his shot and see what would happen. It was hard for him to read her. She wasn't like the other girls in the school, she was focused in class, pretty and didn't have the bitchy attitude that most of the females had.

"Can I join you?" Keith asked sitting down before Lizzy could respond.

"Well sure." Lizzy said taking a drink of the grape soda that came with the school lunch of the day.

"Why are you sitting alone? Where the crew you usually sit with?" Keith asked. He began to nibble at his lunch, the fries were the only edible item on the tray.

"I'm not sure. I'm kind of worried." Lizzy said. She turned to look at the entrance to the cafeteria and then turned back to Keith. "Why are you not sitting with your crew?" She asked smiling. Keith was cute she couldn't deny but he was no Erick and to her, Erick was the best-looking man in the school maybe even the world. The young heart wants what it wants.

Keith shrugged "I don't know where they are. They always go off and do their own thing. I'm used to it though, they're my family."

Before Lizzy could respond Janay ran into the cafeteria and over to the table. "Lizzy, we got to go! It's your sister, she's in trouble."

Lizzy jumped to her feet and followed behind Janay. Keith grabbed his books and noticed Lizzy left hers on the seat next to where she sat. Not thinking twice, he grabbed them and jogged behind Janay and Lizzy until he caught up with them.

The girls came to a stop in front of the principal office where Sabrina sat on the bench being held by Darnell. Sabrina's face was buried in his chest and her crying was muffled. Nearby stood Erick who looked furious. Lizzy rushed over to her sister and Janay was right next to her to comfort her best friend.

"What the hell happened? What is going on?" Lizzy questioned as her sister shifted her body to lay in her Lizzy's shoulder.

Darnell started to speak when the office door opened, and several officers came out leading Sean and Tavon who in handcuffs.

"What are you doing!? Those are my brothers! You can't arrest them!" Keith had the temper of his brother Sean and at that moment he was about to lose it. He didn't know what was happening all he saw was his brothers and in cuffs about to go down to bookings. He looked from them to Sabrina than to the cops than back to his brothers. "Whatever that bitch said she is lying" Keith said walking towards his family and the officers. Lizzy looked at him in shock and before she could say anything to defend her sister Darnell stood to his feet and rushed him.

Darnell was able to get him to the floor and get a few blows to his skull before one of the school security guards pulled them apart. The police officers were busy pulling the suspects away forcefully. They were putting up a fight especially after they saw their little brother on the ground getting beat up. They were all over eighteen and were getting taken down to the station to get questioned but were making their case worse every second they resisted arrest.

***

Sabrina and Lizzy sat in the principal's office and awaited their parents. Outside the office doors were a police officer as well as her friends, who refused to leave until she left.

"What's going on" Christopher asked approaching Darnell who was pacing back and forth outside the office.

Although Darnell and Sabrina were not blood, he thought of her as family and he was ready to kill Sean for putting his hands on her again and for touching his sister. After the first situation that happened almost a year ago, Darnell had been fighting the urge to handle the Sean situation himself. Several attempts of pleading and trying to get Sabrina to press charges went unheeded and he just bit his tongue. Darnell stopped and turned to his old friend Christopher.

Christopher could see the anger in his eyes and the stress he carried in his face. His gaze wandered to the officer posted outside the office door and over to Erick and Janay seated on the bench next to the officer they looked defeated and upset.

"What the hell happened?" Christopher asked again his voice full of concern.

Darnell gestured for Chris to walk with him and so he did. Walking to the other end of the hall Darnell swallowed the lump in his throat. What he was about to ask, what he was about to do was against everything he stood for. Darnell was a changed man, he gave up the street life when he made the promise to his dad on his deathbed. "I need to cash that favor in."

Christopher's eyes widened, he checked his surroundings than stepped closer to Darnell placing a hand on his shoulder. "Whatever you need, I got you." Christopher said before they dabbed each other up and pulling each other into a brotherly hug.

Chapter 5

"Due to the rape happening over a year ago, the best course of action is to present the current charges of sexual assault. The evidence is strong in this. A judge will be less likely to convict these boys of rape due to the lack of evidence and the amount of time that has passed. Although you have the record of abortion there is no record that the act of conceiving that child was consensual or not. It is up to you how you would like to pursue this case these are only my recommendations." The lawyer said as she sat in front of Sabrina and her mom.

Her mom was persistent in trying to get her daughter to press charges after she found out what happened along with Darnell. However, after the abortion Sabrina shut down completely, she barely ate, spoke to anyone or interacted with her family. It was as if her spirit left her body and went to another dimension. Sabrina was just going through the motions. It broke her mom's heart that she could not heal her daughter or take her pain away. Sabrina never spoke about what happened other than she was raped, it wasn't till this day that they sat in the office of their defense lawyer that her mom found out multiple men were involved.

"Is there anything we can do that will cause these monsters to be put away for a long time?" Katherine spoke her voice horse trying to push the words through her tears. It was times like these she prayed for her husband. She missed him dearly. It seemed after his death overseas the family seemed to have a crack and evil just seemed to filter in.

The lawyer cleared her throat as she looked down at her paperwork. "To get them all...no. However..." when that word of hope was spoken Sabrina lifted her head from the floor and looked at the lawyer hopeful as she continued to speak. "...Sean has a record and the judge would be less likely to allow him a slap on the wrist. But sweetie, you will need to testify, we will need to convince the judge that he was the mastermind. You will need to tell everything that happened. Can you do that?" Her attorney sat up in her chair and awaited the answer, she was confident she could obtain a conviction of at least a minimum of two years and a maximum of four for Sean based on his past convictions of assault, domestic violence, possession with intent to sell, grand theft auto, and his current charge of sexual assault. All she needed to do was cause doubt of innocence and the evidence helped tremendously.

Sabrina felt her stomach turn to knots. The thought of having to relive that and the thought of everyone knowing was her fear, but the thought of him getting away with it again superseded that fear. She wiped her eyes and squeezed her mother's hand swallowing the lump in her throat before speaking. "I'll do it."

Chapter 6

The past four weeks had been tough for both Sabrina's friends and family and Keith's. Keith was still attending classes just to get away from the constant bickering him and his mom was getting into. Their mom was a junky and Sean feed her habit and kept the income coming in. With him still in bookings awaiting trial and Tavon on the box for violating probation their mom expected Keith to step up. Money that was saved for living day to day life was now going to pay for Sean's legal fees. Time was ticking, and Keith knew he either had to play ball of he would be out on the streets by his mother's hand.

Keith walked out of the school's locker room dressed in a pair of black denim jeans and Aeropostale logo t-shirt and a fitted baseball cap. He had changed out of his school clothes at the end of school and was on his way to go meet his cousins who were supposed to show him the ins and outs. As he walked through the hall his red backpack hanging from his shoulder he stopped abruptly when he saw Lizzy standing at her locker gathering her belongings. The halls were empty due to school being over, just a few administrators lingered inside their classrooms. Keith filled with rage as he walked towards her.

"Can we talk?" Keith asked. His voice was hard and tense. He was trying his best to keep his anger from erupting the last thing his family needed was two sons in jail. Lizzy turned around and rolled her eyes at the site of him and his jaw tensed at the reaction. She had no reason to feel any type of way he felt, it wasn't her brother sitting in a damn cell.

"We have nothing to discuss. What your brother did to my sister is fucking disgusting and I hope they bury his ass under the jail!" Lizzy didn't know the full story; her mom and sister spared the details of gang rape. To Lizzy, Sean was the only one involved. She had no reservations on speaking how she felt. That was one way she and Sabrina differed. Lizzy was outspoken and the bubbly one and Sabrina was the shy and quiet one.

Keith swallowed the demon inside before he opened his mouth. "She is lying, he's not capable of any of what she's accusing him of" he said through gritted teeth. The action of Lizzy laughing in his face caused his mood to turn completely. Keith could no longer keep his composure. "What the fuck is so funny?" He asked visibly to upset stepping forward a little.

Lizzy didn't intimidate easily. She continued to chuckle as she grabbed her book bag and closed her locker before fixing her attention back on Keith. "You know and I know he did that shit. Your brother's reputation proceeds him. I knew he wasn't shit when she introduced me. Fuck your brother, fuck you and your dysfunctional ass family. Your brother is going to pay." She said her finger in his face to emphasize her words.

Keith invaded her space causing her to back against the lockers before he punched the locker space next to her skull.

He looked straight in her brown eyes and his jaw tensed up before he let out a half chuckle and smirk looking her over and walked away.

Lizzy stood there for a moment frozen watching him walk away till he disappeared around the corner. Her gaze wandered up to the fist imprint that sat next to her locker. Keith had punched the locker so hard it left it dented. Lizzy pulled her backpack on and walked the opposite way towards the exit of the school to meet up with Erick.

***

Erick followed behind Lizzy to her front door. He had been picking her up and taking her home every day since the incident happened with her sister. Sabrina was finishing her senior year out via an online high school, so she didn't need the chauffeur.

"Wait up" Erick said jogging to catch up to his girl before she reached the door. He grabbed her hand gently and pulled her to him. "I got something for you." Erick said pulling out a rectangular box that looked like it could be a necklace or some piece of jewelry.

Lizzy bounced up and down slightly with excitement, Erick admiring the sight. Grabbing the box smiling she opened it to reveal a charm bracelet that spelled the word 'PROM?'.

"I know it's not till next year but it's not too early to ask right?" Erick asked looking unsure if he was doing too much trying to gauge Lizzy's reaction.

She rolled her eyes playfully. "I mean who else are you going to take?" she said jokingly. Erick laughed before he grabbed her waist and pulled her closer to him planting a kiss on her lips just as the front door opened.

Darnell stood there shaking his head. "I knew it!" he said holding his hands up in surrender cracking a smile.

"Oh hush." Lizzy said pushing past him and walking into the house.

Erick attempted to go inside but his brother stopped him.

"Let me talk to you for a second." Darnell said stepping onto the porch closing the door.

"What's up?" Erick asked looking concerned.

Darnell blew out a breath of air before he opened his mouth to say what he needed to say. "I initiated the favor from Christopher." He said looking out onto the street.

Erick didn't say anything he stood there and pondered what his brother just said. "You think that's necessary?" Erick asked his brother.

Christopher and Darnell, we're at one point considered inseparable. When Christopher started going down the street life, joining a gang, getting arrested and moving merchandise Darnell distanced himself a little and Christopher understood. When Christopher needed Darnell and he was capable he was always there for him. The act that created the favor would have caused Christopher to go away for life. His friend was there, and he owed him his life. Although Christopher did some time it didn't amount to what he could have done. The time he spent in jail they stayed in contact, but Christopher always felt like shit for asking his friend to risk it all for him. He promised him if he ever needed anything, he would be there for him and that was their last communication while he was on the inside.

Darnell shrugged as he watched the traffic ride up and down the street. "I don't know bro, but I promised Ms. Katherine a while ago I would watch out for Sabrina and this is the only way I know how. He likes her, and he can protect her, and he's capable of murder we both know that." Darnell said his jaw clenching as he thought about what he did for his friend so long ago. Erick placed a hand on his brother's shoulder and squeezed, he trusted him and was always going to be in his corner before he walked in the house.

***

"What the hell wrong with you?" Mike asked as he dabbed up his little cousin.

"Nothing. I'm good" Keith said as he looked around his surroundings. He had gone home and dropped his bag off before he met up with his cousins at Mondawmin which wasn't that far from his home. At the end of the day, he had to do what he needed to provide for his family, no matter how much he disliked his home situation; it was home. He was doing this more for his brothers than his mom.

The acts of the shadows start under the illumination of the Baltimore street lights. Keith's job was to be the lookout as his cousins executed the sales. After a few days of this, he would be able to get in the trenches and start bringing home a cut, but only after he was approved by Lamar the man who supplied and kingpin of certain dealings of the night in Baltimore City.

After a few hours and the time wined down to almost 2 a.m., Mike and Keith sat in his car in front of Keith's house. Keith glared from the passenger seat of his cousin's car to the rowhouse he called home and sighed deeply. An action not missed by his older cousin.

Mike was nineteen and the mystery of the family. He never stood out in a crowd but commanded respect wherever he went. He could blend with any group of people and although he was a gang member, a hustler he was also much more than that. He kept good grades, was intelligent and knew there was more in life than just being a trap nigga. He finished rolling the blunt and lit it taking a pull from it and handing it to his little cousin. "Things will get better lil cuz" Mike said as if he could read his little cousin's thoughts.

Keith inhaled the Kush and released, coughing a little from the execution. Out of all his siblings and his cousins, Mike was the one person he could talk real with. Be himself and not feel like he had to prove himself. He loved his brothers dearly, but they were street to the core. They didn't see over the struggle or did they try, Tavon and Sean were comfortable and that's where the siblings differed. Where Tavon and Sean's vision stopped, Keith's was expanding. He knew there was more, he wanted more. It just sucked that his inner struggles reflected his outer. "I'm scared man." Keith said to his cousin before he took another pull from the blunt and handed it over.

"Your brother is going to be good. No matter what goes down…" Mike said before he was interrupted by Keith.

"I'm not scared of that. I'm scared of myself!" Mike quieted and took a pull from the blunt allowing his little cousin to finish. "Sometimes I feel like this darkness, anger, another person is inside of me scratching to get out, and I'm tired of fighting" Keith paused and looked at his cousin. "I'm afraid that once I stop fighting, I'm going to like that other person."

Mike had put the blunt out and shifted in his seat to give his little cousin his full attention. "I get it. Believe me, I get it, but whatever you do, keep fighting." He pulled his little cousin into a hug and held him tightly.

***

Keith sat down on the metal stool in front of the glass window and awaited his brother. He made it his mission to go see his brother at the city jail every visiting day if he could. By him being the only one in the family without a record he was the only one permitted to visit him. The iron door buzzed, and his brother walked in dressed in a blue jumpsuit, Sean made his way over to his brother and sat on the other side of the glass. He seemed to be in better spirits than the last visit and that was apparent from the smile on his face. They picked up the phone that was hanging next to them at just the same time. "Man, I'm happy to see you." Sean said shifting in his seat trying to get as comfortable as possible.

Keith exhaled a sigh of annoyance before he opened his mouth to address his older brother. "So why you do it?" Keith asked directly. As much as he tried to convince himself, and others that his brother was innocent the sad truth was he knew his brother. He knew his narcissistic tendencies and stupidity made him act without thinking.

Sean brows tilted into a frown as he looked through the partition at his little brother. "Seriously, you're going to ask me that? I may have assaulted her, but I didn't rape that little bitch. It was consensual. What you believe her over your own blood?" Sean said into the phone as he tried to keep calm.

Keith didn't say anything just, yet he just looked at his brother, looked at his surroundings then cleared his throat. "That's what I told her little sister" Keith didn't go into detail due to the conversation being recorded. "Sorry bro, I just had to ask for peace of mind. Moms have been riding my ass, I haven't been thinking straight. What is your lawyer talking about?" Keith asked. He saw Sean's anger dissipate a little and a slight smile came back across his face.

"A slap on the wrist the worst two to three years, due to my priors." Sean said.

Keith's eyes widened. He couldn't understand why his brother was smiling, that was a long ass time. "Does he still want you to plead guilty?" he asked concerned.

"Yeah but only because if it goes to trail, I can go away for six or more years...." Sean saw the disappointment on his little brother's face and touched the glass. "Whatever mom have you doing, don't get caught up in it. You're the one that is supposed to make it out, go to college and make something out of yourself. When Tavon off his box, run from this life as fast as you can." Sean said his voice full of conviction. Keith matched his brother's hand against the glass partition and nodded his head before they dropped their hands to the side. The brother's talked until the visit was over then said their goodbyes.

Keith walked out of the jail and over to the car where Mike sat waiting for him. Mike had a domestic violence charge on him which hindered him from visiting his cousin. "How is he?" Mike asked as he turned the key in the ignition and the car roared to life.

Keith fastened his seat belt and leaned back in the seat. "He going to do time. How much depends on if he pleads guilty." Keith said looking out the window at the prison that sat in the middle of the city of Baltimore.

Mike pulled off processing what his little cousin just said to him. As they sat at the red light, he contemplated his next move and his next words carefully. "I want to show you something." He said before stepping on the gas and heading in the opposite direction of Keith's house.

Chapter 7

The place Mike took Keith was unexpected. Mike parked the car and they sat in silence for a few seconds until the silence was broken by Keith.

"What are we doing at a cemetery?" Keith asked with concern in his voice as he sat up in his seat and looked around. His eyes rested on his older cousin who sat frozen in the driver's seat staring straight, the act scared him a little he never saw Mike afraid.

Mike pulled back into reality and undid his seat belt. "Get out." He said not even looking in the direction of his little cousin.

Keith didn't hesitate he was scared and curious, he joined his cousin out the car and caught up with him. Mike was slowly walking towards an unknown destination.

"You have a choice to make, and that choice will affect everyone around your current and future" Mike stopped and turned toward his cousin looking him right in the eyes. "This street life will get you two places. Dead or Prison. You at this moment can be whatever you want to be, do whatever you want to do. Your brothers and I discussed this from time to time. The time when you would have to choose…" Mike trailed off.

"Why are we having this talk in a cemetery?" Keith asked.

Mike crouched down to the grave they stood in front and wiped the leaves from it unveiling the name Brandon Turner. Keith still looked confused. Mike stood back up and released a sigh. "Meet my son, Brandon Turner." Mike's voice cracked as he tried to hold back the flood of emotions going through him.

Keith's eyes widened in shock as he took in what his cousin just said. He never knew he had a child. "What happened, when, how?" Keith was full of questions which was understandable. Mike had a way of hiding aspects of his life from his own family. Only Sean and Tavon knew of his son and what happened that led to his death. His own mom didn't even know she had a grandchild.

"Like I said this life affects everyone around you, current and future." Mike said staring down at his four-year-old son's grave. "My choices are why my son lays here today. The streets are an addicting, dangerous and unforgiving place. A drive by took my son from me, a stupid gang rivalry." Mike said as he began to cry. Keith placed his hand on his cousin's shoulder. "Your brother's and I made our choice and I refuse to have you out here. Fuck my aunt and what she wants!" Mike grabbed his little cousin and pulled him into a hug. "I want you to go far away from here, go to college and never look back. Let me and your brothers worry about life here." Keith hugged his older cousin until he finished crying on his shoulder.

***

Keith awoke the following Monday dreading going to school, but he knew he had to. After his cousin revealed his secret to him and bared his soul, he felt this new desire to prove them right. His brother's and cousin that he could break the cycle. However, looking at the snowfall from last night he was dreading going out in it.

Keith walked into the kitchen to his brother Tavon smearing butter on the toast.

"Morning" Keith greeted him as he walked over to the refrigerator to see what he could eat quick.

"What's up?" Tavon asked before taking a bite of his toast.

Keith sighed slamming the refrigerator shut. "Why is there never any food in here?" he said annoyed.

Tavon shrugged as he pulled a knot of money out of his pocket and sat it on the counter. "See if Mike will take you to the market after school." Tavon said. Although he was housebound, he still had his way of making money. Keith grabbed the stack of money and proceeded out the door.

"Bring me my change back!" Tavon yelled behind him playfully before the door slammed shut.

***

It seemed the new hot spot was Sabrina's place since she was now being homeschooled. She enjoyed not having to go out in the cold of winter to commute to school, but she did hate that she wasn't going to have the same senior experience as her friends.

The friends sat around the basement the T.V. watching them, talking and making plans for Halloween which was quickly approaching. Lizzy and Erick sat on the recliner, Lizzy on his lap and Erick's arms around her waist. It was safe to say they were no longer hiding anything, not that anyone cared they all were aware of one another's 'secret' crush.

"I really am not trying to go out in this fidget cold and freeze my butt off." Lizzy said as they all laughed in agreement. Erick squeezed her ass slightly.

"Definitely can't have that." He said smiling looking up at his girl.

"Nigga you corny as hell." Darnell interjected bursting out in laughter. Sabrina who was seated next to him punched him in the arm playfully while Erick gave him the finger.

"I think it's cute." Sabrina said smiling at the new couple. "Lizzy's right though, it's way too cold to go out."

"Well our house will be free Halloween weekend, why don't we just throw a little party there?" Janay said finally pulling herself away from her text messages and joining the conversation. Darnell and Erick shrugged, the idea wasn't bad, and it wasn't like it would be a huge party and the house would be destroyed. Janay bounced up and down in her seat excited about the thought of costume shopping.

***

Lizzy and Sabrina's mom didn't hesitate to let them go over her friend's house for the weekend. She trusted them like her own children. The house was lightly decorated with

Halloween decorations the staircase covered in faux spider webs, a fog machine that cascaded faux fog throughout the main floor and some other novelty decorations throughout the house. Darnell was in the process of filling the plastic witch cauldron with ice and soda's when Erick walked in the house with the girls. No one was dressed in their costumes yet and everyone wasn't there yet.

"I need help!" Janay screamed down the steps from her bedroom. She was struggling with her costume and was frustrated.

"Well, best friend duties call." Sabrina chuckled as she and Lizzy headed to Janay's bedroom to help and dress themselves.

The boys were in full costume by eight and like always were waiting on the girls to be done getting ready. "You would think we were going out with how long it's taking them." Darnell laughed. He walked over to the Bose Bluetooth speaker and turned it on, linking it to his playlist on his phone.

TI's 'What you know' sounded through the speakers. The knock on the door alerted the brothers as Erick went to answer it. Not knowing who it was he looked through the peephole and chuckled to himself, before pulling the door open. As soon as Darnell saw Kayla a big smile came across his face. "Hope you don't mind one extra." Christopher said as he walked over and dabbed up Darnell. Darnell didn't take his eyes off Kayla. "No problem at all."

Kayla wore a cute little girls scout costume complete with white knee-high socks and a cute hat. She smiled at Darnell before making her way over to the cauldron of drinks. "Move it, ladies, everyone's waiting on y'all." Erick yelled up the stairs.

"Everyone?" Sabrina asked aloud looking confused. She was unaware of any other people coming.

Christopher made his way over to Erick who was posted at the bottom landing of the stairs. Erick didn't hesitate to ask what was on his mind.

"Will this favor come back to haunt my brother?" Erick asked directing his full attention to Christopher.

Christopher's jaw clenched. "I owe your brother my life. I won't betray him." Christopher said. He was telling the truth, he had no intent in doing any harm to Darnell. If it wasn't for him, he would still be in jail.

The interaction was cut short when the girls appeared at the top of the staircase. They all wore matching black latex bodysuits paired with black go-go styled boots. Making their way down the steps Erick's eyes were locked onto Lizzy and his hormones were going crazy. Christopher's eyes traveled up and down Sabrina's costume. He was intoxicated by her since the first day she walked into his job.

Once Lizzy and Janay hit the bottom landing, they all split up and went to their dates leaving Christopher and Sabrina standing awkwardly at the bottom of the steps.

"So, where's Robin, Batman?" Sabrina asked Christopher referring to his choice of costume. Feeling as if she spoke him up Janay came darting through the entryway and James followed dressed in his best Robin costume. Christopher and Sabrina burst out into laughter before heading toward the living room to join the party. Upon second glance they realized everyone was coupled up. Darnell and Kayla, Lizzy and Erick, James and Janay.

"Look like your stuck with Batman." Christopher said in his best Batman voice. Sabrina chuckled as she walked away and went over to the snack table.

Looking out into the small party Sabrina felt normal. She felt like a teenager, free of the scars she carried outside the walls of this house. Everyone was dressed in costumes her and the girls were 'Charlie's Angel's', Kayla was a girl's scout, Christopher was Batman, James was Robin and Darnell was a vampire. Sabrina took it all in and vowed that at least tonight she would forget her problems and embrace being someone else.

'Bobby Valentino's Slow Down' sounded through the speakers and the duo's hit the floor for some touch dancing. Christopher eased his way over to Sabrina lifting his mask to reveal his face.

"Who are you supposed to be?" he asked creating small talk.

"Charlie's Angel" Sabrina said posing for the dramatic affect her hands in the air like guns. Christopher chuckled.

"Well would Charlie's Angel like to dance?" he asked smiling.

"Why not?" Sabrina said as she grabbed Christopher's hand and pulled him to the middle of the living room floor which was converted to the temporary dance floor for the moment. It felt everyone was in their own little world even when the song changed to something upbeat. Christopher's hand rested on the small of Sabrina's back as her arms draped on his shoulders.

"So, Batman is a great choice for you." Sabrina said smiling up at Christopher shyly.

"Really? Why is that?" Christopher asked intrigued.

"Well Batman is kind of a character of mystery, and you sir hold a mystery behind those eyes." Sabrina said.

Christopher pulled her a little closer. "Well, your costume fits you also" he said licking his lips. "Your strong, independent, and can definitely fill out a catsuit." Christopher said as they both laughed.

The party ended up turning into a movie night. Everyone was spread out through the living room, some stretched on the L-shaped sofa while Christopher and James rested on the floor. Before she joined her friends in slumber, Sabrina smiled at her surroundings and friends before she closed her eyes leaving the movie to watch them.

Chapter 8

The trial against Sean was due to take place the first week of December. Sabrina and her mom sat in their lawyer's office ready to hear if Sean was going to plead guilty. In her heart she wanted Sean to plead guilty to spare her from having to take the stand.

"It looks like he is pleading guilty." The lawyer said smiling.

The relief that washed over Sabrina felt amazing. Sean was going away as he deserved, and she did not have to relive the horrors by taking the stand.

"How much time will he get?" Sabrina asked. Her mom hugged her as she saw the relief wash over Sabrina.

"Minimum eighteen months" her lawyer said. "I know it's not a lot, but he is serving time for the assault at the school, not the rape. I'm sorry more time couldn't be given." the lawyer looked apologetic. Sabrina smiled, she understood and the fact he was going away at all was good enough for her. No more looking over her shoulders, no more moving around school with uncertainty. Sean was removed from her life and she couldn't be happier.

***

Christopher and Darnell's relationship seemed to pick up where they left off. They had both grown to be better men although they each had a past that many chose to define them as. Christopher grew to get used to being referred to as the felon, the trouble maker, a gangbanger. However, he also made it a mission to never let his past define the future. The boys found themselves sitting in the mall parking lot waiting for Christopher's sister Kayla to get off work.

"So, when did this little thing with my sister start?" Christopher asked chuckling. He had no reservations about it but like a good big brother, he needed to know Darnell's intentions.

Darnell laughed out of embarrassment. Who would have thought him, and Kayla would turn into something? The shy girl that barely said two words to him once she started living with her dad and brothers a year ago. She always stayed to herself whenever Darnell would come around to kick it with Christopher. His trail was the last time he saw the old Kayla. This Kayla had new found confidence with just a hint of shyness and that peaked Darnell's interest. She was no longer socially awkward towards him and he was thankful for that.

Kayla slid into the backseat behind her brother Christopher. "Thanks for picking me up Darnell." She said looking over at him from the backseat.

Darnell looked back at her and smiled, sending her hormones racing. "No problem, anytime" he said as he put the car in reverse and backed out of the parking spot. The car ride was awkward and annoying for Christopher, who found himself in the middle of a boo loving text frenzy between his little sister and Darnell. The chimes coming from one another's cell phone finally pushed Christopher to the boiling point.

"Yo! Focus on the road before you kill us!" Christopher barked with irritation from the passenger seat.

"Mind your business." Kayla said before sending another text causing Darnell's phone to chime again, and her brother to sigh in frustration.

Darnell continued to drive avoiding the urge to pick up his cell phone and reply. "So how was work Kayla?" he asked aloud.

Christopher sucked his teeth. "Like you don't already know." he said before laughing.

***

The knock on the front door alerted Sabrina's mom who was in the kitchen fixing dinner for her and the girls. To her surprise, a handsome young man stood on the opposite side of the door. He stood 5'10", wore a black bubble coat, a pair of black True Religion jeans and black Nike Boots. The snowflakes laid a top of his blonde-tipped afro and slowly melted away as quickly as they fell in place.

"Excuse me, Ms. Moore, my name is Christopher, and I'm a friend of Sabrina's from school. "Christopher finally said. Ms. Moore looked him over before calling for her oldest daughter. Sabrina emerged from her room and replaced her mom at the door. Sabrina blushed a little when she saw who was standing there.

"Hi." She said leaning her body on the door seal her arms folded trying to combat the winter air.

"Hi…" Christopher said as he opened the paper bag under his arm and pulled out a box of hot cocoa and a crappy holiday romance movie from the Redbox. "…I know you said you wouldn't go out with me, but could I join you for a movie and some cocoa?" Christopher said smiling. Sabrina moved aside allowing him entry before closing and locking the door.

"I'll be right back, go into the living room." Sabrina said. As she walked into the kitchen her mom stopped what she was doing and gave her a smile.

"Living Room only!" she said waving her finger. Sabrina gave her mom a kiss on the cheek then went back to Christopher.

Christopher had come out his coat and was seated in the living room, his face lit up when he saw Sabrina.

"Where's the movie and coco?" Sabrina asked walking towards him. Christopher gave her the items then leaned back on the sofa. Sabrina proceeded to start the movie than excited to the kitchen to make the hot beverages, before returning to her movie date.

***

Christopher and Sabrina became close the last three weeks of November, he even helped the Moore's decorate for Christmas, along with Erick of course, and made an appearance on Thanksgiving. Christopher and Sabrina sat in his room laid across the bed talking.

Sabrina felt different with Christopher. They never defined what they were or either shared a kiss with one another, they were friends. Christopher never made Sabrina feel like she needed to be anything other than who she was. She could be her damaged, vulnerable self and not feel judged. Who was Christopher to judge her, when the skeletons in his closet piled up and were burying him? He of all people knew the need and desire of just having someone that could relate to the fear of being judged and holding a secret.

"Can I ask you something?" Sabrina asked as she stared up at the ceiling.

Christopher swallowed the lump in his throat. "Sure." he said.

"Why were you in jail?" Sabrina asked.

Christopher chuckled, he knew that question was going to come up sooner than later.

"I was wondering when you were going to ask. I was charged with possession, robbery, and assault with a deadly weapon, but that was dropped." He said.

"Why was it dropped?" Sabrina asked sitting up to face Christopher who was still laid on his back.

Christopher looked over at her. "The weapon was never found." Christopher said watching her body's response to his answer. He knew he could elaborate more but that would mean incriminating Darnell, and that was something he was not prepared to do.

Sabrina bit her lip as she looked at Christopher. She wanted to know everything, but she knew if she started digging, he would too. And she wasn't ready to answer those questions just yet.

"Will you come with me tomorrow?" Sabrina asked. She didn't have to be there, but she wanted to look in the eyes of the monster that traumatized her dreams and took her innocence. She wanted to see them haul him away and the bondage he was now faced to live in. Although it was nothing compared to her emotional bondage.

Christopher sat up until they were face to face. "I will be there right by your side." He said. Sabrina's gaze wandered from Christopher's, but he didn't falter.

"This may be out of line and feel free to smack the shit out of me if it is, but can I kiss you?" Christopher asked. The nervousness ever so present in his voice.

Sabrina looked up a small hint of a smile crept on her face. She breathed in deeply before she responded. "Yes." she said as their eyes locked. Christopher brought his lips to Sabrina's, remaining inches from her lips before he went in for the kiss.

Chapter 9

It was on Sabrina's mind heavy that day. Her nerves were at her worst, but her support was right by her side. Mom, sister and lawyer. The courtroom was full of tension from both sides. Sean's side was filled with the four men that always stood by him Mike, Tavon, Keith and Chad.

The sound of chains alerted Sabrina to the impending approach of the villain of a story, Sean. One last breath and the door is opened. Shawn's eyes scanned the courtroom until they finally came to a rest on Sabrina. As hard as it was to stare in the eyes of Sean Sabrina fought the urge to look away, she wanted him to know he no longer had power over her.

Quick and easy, the trail went. Sean plead guilty to sexual assault and attempted rape and was sentenced to twenty-four months in prison. *'Bang, Bang'* the gavel went. Sabrina, her mom, and sister embraced each other in a hug, relief and satisfaction washing over them. Christopher and

Darnell stood behind them watching the sheriff take Sean back to the bullpen. The gesture was settle and slight but both Darnell and Christopher caught it. The subtle head nod between Sean and his brother, and the scowl Tavon gave Sabrina before him and Keith exited the courtroom.

"You saw that?" Darnell asked Christopher.

Christopher's jaw clenched as he watched them disappear behind the courtroom doors. "Yeah. He's going to be a problem." Christopher said.

***

This winter seemed to be harsher than previous winters in Baltimore. Schools seemed to be closed at least three times a week due to below freezing temperatures or the snow falls that left piles of cold white fluff behind.

Keith sat in his bedroom, shades and curtains shut smoking a blunt. His struggle with his living situation was becoming a whole new level of toxicity. Weed and school were his only safe havens. Weed provided the mental release and school provided the physical. Having to be confined to the hell of his house due to the weather and nowhere to go was a test for the *'Mr. Hyde'* hiding behind the surface.

He pulled on the joint one last time before putting it out on the side of his dresser. Keith pulled his body off the bed and walked reluctantly to his closed bedroom door. The muffled voices on the other side of the door sent a surge of anger through him before he turned the doorknob and walked into the chaos of his home.

***

Christmas time in the hood is a time for laughs, friends, and family. It's also a time of masks, disappointments, and heartache. Sabrina and Lizzy's mom spent Christmas eve wrapping gifts in her room while the girls were spending the evening with their friends, well boyfriends.

"I'm not doing this." Christopher said laughing. He looked surprised and horrified that Sabrina brought him to an ice-skating rink. Couples and a few teenagers danced across the ice like pros, with a few hugging the wall trying not to fall.

Sabrina handed him his skates and sat down on the bench to get her skates on. Christopher sat back on the bench and just watched her and the ice.

"You really about to go out there?" Christopher asked with a curious grin as he watched her tie the laces of the skates. He enjoyed her company a lot. Sabrina was different from the round the way chicks. She had genuine innocence to her, and he was exposed to new things that he knew he would probably never been exposed to with another girl. Sabrina smiled at him and shook her head.

"No. We are going out there." Sabrina patted him on the leg before heading towards the ice.

Christopher sucked up his pride as he clenched the wall trying to hold himself up. Sabrina skated over to him laughing at the sight of Christopher trying to balance on the ice. "You're going to have to let the wall go." Sabrina said amused.

"Nope. No, I don't." Christopher was out of his element and it was apparent. Sabrina found it amusing.

Sabrina didn't expect him to even come on the ice and was impressed. She pulled him into a kiss which eased Christopher's nerves some. "Thanks for trying. Let's get out of here." Sabrina said.

***

Tavon was off the box and back to bringing in the money and supply for their mom. Although things didn't go back to normal for Keith. It seemed his mom got off on being emotionally abusive to him and belittling him every chance she got. Most of the time she was high when she wasn't high, she was sleep. Christmas was no different if anything it was worst.

Keith and Tavon sat in the living room with a blunt in a rotation when Keith broke the silence. "Mike took me to the grave." He said passing the blunt back to his brother.

"Good you should know what happened to your little cousin." Tavon said taking a drag on the blunt.

"You need to cut mom off." Keith said.

Tavon chuckled "Are you crazy? Mom would kick us both out." he said.

"No, she won't. That would require her to get a fucking job to pay her own bills." Keith said taking the blunt from his brother. "You know I never saw her sober. Do you know how fucked up that shit is? Just think about it, bro." Keith said he heard the footsteps coming from his mother's room and decided to retreat to his before it was too late. He passed the blunt back to his brother "Merry Christmas." he said before retreating to the safety of his room.

***

'5,4,3,2,1, Happy New Year!' the ball dropped all around the world and life went on for everyone in Baltimore. Nothing new, no cliché new year's resolutions, just the routine that everyone had grown accustomed to.

Everyone was coupled up and happy. Sabrina felt normal, she felt safe and happy for once. She no longer had to look over her shoulder or think about the worst-case scenario. The new school year was starting, and Prom season was right around the corner. All that needed to be decided was the colors they each would wear.

Sabrina laid in Christopher's arms in his full-sized bed as they talked about to upcoming prom. "I can't believe school is just about over." Sabrina said. She was right it was time to apply to college and prepare for the next chapters in their life.

"Don't forget about me when you go off to college." Christopher said jokingly. Chris kissed her on the cheek before he got up from the bed grabbing his shirt and pulling it over his head. Sabrina and Christopher had yet to take their relationship to the physical side, yet they had become close and comfortable with each other.

Sabrina watched Christopher pull his t-shirt over his tattooed muscular frame. She liked what she saw and as fast as the rush of hormones came running through her, so did the voice of criticism. The voice that caused her to second guess herself, made her feel small and abnormal and caused her body to tense and her gaze to drop from Christopher.

Christopher didn't miss the change in Sabrina's body language, he had been noticing it a lot more lately. He walked over and sat on the edge of his bed. "Come here, Bre." he said softly. Sabrina sat up and scooted closer to Christopher on the edge of the bed. "I won't hurt you." Christopher said looking over at Sabrina who was kicking her dangling feet off the side of the bed.

"That's what he said." Sabrina blurted out.

The silence sat between them for a moment before Christopher broke it. "You have to forget that if you're ever going to live a happy life. You can't take what he did out on every guy you're going to be with. "

Sabrina looked at him and the concern in his eyes broke her heart. Christopher was right, and he never made her feel anything but safe when she was with him, but Sabrina was still apprehensive about taking things to another level. "You're right, but I can't forget it. I keep getting a haunting feeling that it's going to happen again."

"He's locked up, and I won't let anything happen to you. Maybe if you get it off your chest and talk about it, you'll feel more comfortable around me." Christopher said grabbing Sabrina's hand gently and giving it a slight squeeze for reassurance.

Sabrina looked at Christopher questionably. "You really want to know what happened?" Christopher shook his head, yes and Sabrina swallowed the lump in her throat.

"*I remember it like it was yesterday. I remember their smell and voices. I remember waking up and my body was heavy, and vision was blurry. I felt like I wasn't in control of my body, I couldn't move. I heard someone coming downstairs.*

He came over and started running his hand up my skirt, and I started screaming. A hand across the face stopped me and he told me to shut up. I tried so hard to move my body, it felt like I was paralyzed. I heard more footsteps come down the steps and tape went over my mouth."

Sabrina started to cry, she hadn't told the details of that day to anyone other than her lawyer. "They took my virginity. When they were done, they threatened to kill me if I told the police. They dropped me off home and left." She looked at Christopher wiping her face.

"I'm sorry you went through that." Christopher said wiping Sabrina's face. He was flushed with anger and hate for the boys that did that to her. Christopher pulled her into a hug not knowing what else to say, he just wanted to protect her.

Chapter 10

Prom Season.

Keith walked out his mom's house in his rented tuxedo feeling like a million bucks. He decided to enjoy his night and party his worries away. "I'm most likely going to go to the after party, but I will hit you up when I'm ready." Keith said.

"Have fun." Mike said reaching over and pulling a three-pack box of condoms from his glove compartment. "Always be prepared" Mike said smiling. Keith slid them in his pocket chuckling and exited the car.

Keith walked into the venue and breathed in the fantasy of prom. The fancy dresses, the dressed up young men, the music of his generation on the stereos. He felt like someone new and tonight he was going to embrace the fantasy of junior prom.

***

"Sure, I can't escort you? I can just wear my tux for my senior prom." Erick said as he sat behind the driver's seat in front of the haul. Lizzy wanted to do the junior prom with her new friends and senior prom with her boyfriend.

Lizzy leaned over and kissed him softly on the lips. "Senior prom I'm all yours. Tonight, is about me and my friends. I'll text you when I'm ready to go home baby." Lizzy said as she jumped from the passenger seat and headed into the prom.

The night carried on smoothly. Lizzy and her friends danced to the bangers the DJ played and took an undocumented number of selfies. Keith was enjoying himself to, anytime outside his house was a good time for him. Keith sat in his chair eating when Lizzy caught his eye. He hadn't been this close to her since their back and forth in the school hallway months ago. He was sort of blackballed by his classmates after the information of the trail came to light, everyone of course sided with Sabrina and anyone associated

with Sean was just as bad. So, Keith just sat and ate and

observed, and danced in his seat a little he didn't mind being

alone.

He was second guessing the after party and wanted to

leave but dreaded going home. The prom king and queen was

about to be crowned and he felt it would be now or never if he

was going to call it a night. Keith texted Mike then grabbed his

jacked before slipping out the ballroom. To his surprise Lizzy

was standing by the entrance with her phone in her hand

looking beautiful in her black and white bodycon dress. Keith

reluctantly walked up to the exit and stood across from her, the

awkwardness thick in the air until it was broken with

conversation.

"Leaving so soon?" Lizzy asked. She kind of felt bad for

Keith, before all of this he seemed like a decent guy. She

noticed how his mood shifted and people's moods towards him

shifted after everything and she felt bad. He wasn't his brother and like her, he was just finding out what happened the same time she was.

"Yeah. I don't know why I came honestly." Keith said coldly. He took a deep breath. "I'm sorry about the whole locker thing and losing my cool." Keith said finally meeting Lizzy's eyes. Her gaze was warm and welcoming with a hint of pity. He looked at his phone to check if Mike had hit him up, he didn't. "I'm sorry about what my brother did to your sister." Keith said his voice cracking a little causing him to clear his throat.

Lizzy phone chimed and she cleared her throat. "Thank you for saying that. You look nice by the way." Lizzy said cracking a smile as she pushed the door open and headed towards Erick's car.

"Yeah, you look nice too." Keith said as he watched her climb into the car.

***

Tavon and his cousin Chad pulled up across the street from Sabrina's house and killed the engine.

"You sure about this Tavon?" Chad asked as he stared impatiently at the house.

"Positive, this is for Sean." Tavon said. He was far from being in his right mind since he started sniffing dope like his mother the past month and Chad was down for anything unlawful.

***

"Darnell, I'm staying with Sabrina tonight." Janay said as she retired back from the kitchen to the living room with a bottle of water.

"Okay. We'll be pass in the morning. Darnell said leaving the house.

Christopher pulls Sabrina into a kiss and squeezes her butt playfully. "I'll be pass tomorrow beautiful" He said smiling. James and Christopher leave the house and get in the car.

***

Lizzy and Erick sat in the car in front of a *'Motel 6'*.

"Are you sure about this?" Erick asked looking over at Lizzy

who was sitting in the passenger seat looking nervous.

"I'm ready and I want it to be with you." Lizzy said

meeting Erick's eyes and smiling.

***

Back at home things were about to take a turn for the

worst. Vengeance is destructive to everyone involved. Tavon

and Chad exited the car and walked up to the front door and

knocked. The door swung open with Janay standing there in

shock, she thought it was the boys coming back because they

forgot something. She attempted to push the door closed and

lock it, but it was too late. Tavon punched her in the face

causing her to fall to the ground and they walked into

Sabrina's home closing and locking the door behind them.

Chad and Tavon went through the house like a tornado,

leaving destruction behind everywhere they touched. Sabrina

sat forcefully on her knees with a fist full of hair wrapped in Chad's fist watching Tavon beat on her best friend. Janay and Tavon had a history between one another, he was always abusive, but the dope was enhancing it. He was like a pot left to long on the burner and was boiling over. All the pain and hurt he felt he delivered through blow after blow to Janay's body and face. Making Sabrina watch was the icing on the cake he wanted her to feel the pain he felt everyday not having his brother home with him, he was determined.

The cries and screams coming from Sabrina were muted by his rage until he finally threw the final blow that rendered Janay unconscious. Tavon stood drenched in sweat and breathing rapidly. "This is on you! You took someone I loved, and I returned the favor!" Tavon said. He laughed to himself before delivering a punch to the face of Sabrina. Chad released her and her body fell straight to the floor next to her best friends.

***

Mike hung up the phone and breathed in deeply. He was frustrated and pissed after getting a collect call from the city jail, from his cousin Tavon. Tavon told him one thing, to look out for Keith.

Mike's frustration was apparent on his face when he walked back into the living room where Keith sat. "What's wrong with you?" Keith asked. He was shuffling the deck of Uno cards when he saw the state Mike was in and stopped.

Mike's jaw clenched as he bit his tongue trying to filter the words that was about to come out his mouth. "That was Tavon. He's locked up."

Keith felt himself get hot as if his blood was boiling inside him. He had yet to respond to what his cousin just told him, and Mike was standing a few feet away awaiting a reaction. Suddenly it was as if a switched turned on in Keith. He clenched his jaw, took a few deep breaths and continued to shuffle the deck of cards.

The action unsettled Mike even more. "Yo cuz, you heard what I said?" Mike asked just to be sure. He was expecting some kind of reaction, not none.

Keith looked at his older cousin with a coldness in his eyes that he had never seen. "Yeah. I heard you." Keith said as he started dealing the cards. "You are playing or not?" he asked.

***

Sabrina was awake but still confined to a hospital bed. "How's Janay?" she asked. Her words were directed to everyone in the room which was her sister and mom. She hoped it was good news, she prayed it was good news.

Sabrina's mom squeezed her daughters' hand. "Just rest sweetie. The police got them. I'm so sorry…" Sabrina's mom was cut off by her daughter.

"Mom don't! This isn't your fault. Now how is Janay?" Sabrina asked again her voice sterner. The silence was gut wrenching.

"She hasn't woken up yet. Her families with her sweetheart and we're praying for her." Sabrina's mom said as tears filled her eyes. Sabrina started to cry herself. Thinking about how her best friend could be dying and blaming herself once again. Lizzy didn't say anything she just stood by her oldest sister's bedside holding her hand and thinking if she was there just maybe she could have done something to help.

Sabrina

Excerpt from book two

One year to the day. I sat in my dorm room at Capitol college looking at photos of Janay and me. She was still in a coma and had yet to wake up and although time had moved forward, I still carried around the blame from that day.

'Knock Knock'

The sound on the dorm room door summoned me and broke her out of the trance I was in. Christopher stood on the other side of the door with an overnight bag across his shoulders and a smile.

"Did you forget I was coming?" Christopher said walking into the room. He threw his backpack onto the bed then walked over to give me a proper greeting. "You look stressed. That's why I didn't sign up for this school shit." he said laughing.

I gave him a playful push. "You have no idea what you're missing." she said biting down on her lip. We had started being intimate right after graduation and I seemed to develop a craving for it every time we were alone together.

Christopher didn't miss the devilish look in her eyes as he smiled one back. "You a freak." he said pulling his shirt off to reveal his artwork of a torso. Christopher was a gym rat and a health nut, and his hard work was visible.

"You like it though." locking the door I ran and jumped into my man's arms as we began to make out falling onto the twin sized bed.

***

Lizzy

"Yo Lizzy wait up!" Keith yelled after me spotting me in the school parking lot. I stopped and allowed him to catch up. "The final project for history. You alright working with me, right? I mean I don't want to stir up any trouble." Keith said tugging on his backpack that hung off his shoulder.

A horn honked and I knew it was Erick. "Let me think on it. I'll have a definite answer by Monday." I said. I honestly didn't know what to say. Yes, he was related to the monsters that terrorized my sister, but you can't demonize someone on just being related to the devil. Can you? Waving bye I ran over to Ericks car.

"What the hell was that? What he want?" Erick asked being protective of me. He still felt guilt he wasn't there to protect his sister and unlike me he chose to label Keith's whole family as monsters including him.

"We suppose to work together on this final project. He was seeing if I was okay with that." I said.

The car came to a stop at the red light and Erick gripped the wheel tighter than ever. He was mad, no more like pissed. "Are you freaking kidding me Lizzy? This boy's brothers assaulted your sister and mines and you're talking about working with him!?" Erick continued to drive.

"His brother's not him, and I told him I would have to think about it. You yelling at me and treating me like a fucking child is not going to help my decision. You need to chill out. How about saying 'hi' first instead of giving me the third degree." I said.

The rest of the car ride was in silence and when Erick put the car in park, I wasted no time slamming the car door behind me as I went into the house. Things had been rough ever since the accident for our relationship. Erick tolerance grew shorter and my loving and forgiving nature seemed to be the spark. We argued a lot more and had sex a lot less, but at the root we did love each other. Erick sat there for a few minutes before he

drove away pissed.

***

Made in the USA
Coppell, TX
22 April 2022